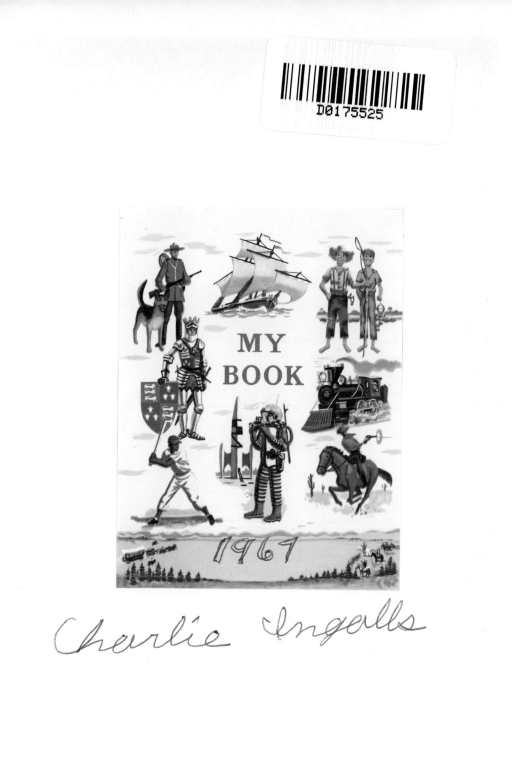

MY BOOK

1964

Charlie Ingalls

Books by Jim Kjelgaard

BIG RED

REBEL SIEGE

FOREST PATROL

BUCKSKIN BRIGADE

CHIP, THE DAM BUILDER

FIRE HUNTER

IRISH RED

KALAK OF THE ICE

A NOSE FOR TROUBLE

SNOW DOG

THE STORY OF GERONIMO

STORMY

COCHISE, CHIEF OF WARRIORS

TRAILING TROUBLE

THE EXPLORATIONS OF PERE MARQUETTE

THE SPELL OF THE WHITE STURGEON

WILD TREK

OUTLAW RED

THE LOST WAGON

THE COMING OF THE MORMONS

LION HOUND

CRACKER BARREL TROUBLE SHOOTER

TRADING JEFF AND HIS DOG

DESERT DOG

HAUNT FOX

THE OKLAHOMA LAND RUN

DUCK-FOOTED HOUND

DOUBLE CHALLENGE

SWAMP CAT

THE LAND IS BRIGHT

RESCUE DOG OF THE HIGH PASS

HI JOLLY!

WOLF BROTHER

WILDLIFE CAMERAMAN

ULYSSES AND HIS WOODLAND ZOO

TIGRE

FAWN IN THE FOREST AND OTHER WILD ANIMAL STORIES

TWO DOGS AND A HORSE

WEEKLY READER CHILDREN'S BOOK CLUB

presents

TWO DOGS AND A HORSE

by Jim Kjelgaard

ILLUSTRATED BY SAM SAVITT

Dodd, Mead & Company, New York

Contents

A Dog Remembers

This is the story of a friendly, amiable dog who became a victim of man's hasty judgment. Although compelled to live as the wild live, he clung to the memory of a gentle old man. A judgment of death was passed upon him, and the crack of a rifle and a red-hot bullet burning his ribs were his farewell salutes from all he had known. But he never forgot the comradeship of a human voice and the touch of a human hand, and from this came a fidelity great er than his heritage from the wild, fierce packs with which his ancestors had once hunted.

The dog came out of the hills one morning with old Jed Fentress and walked beside him into the town of Stauffer. Jed carried a shepherd's crook, although, so far as anyone knew, he had never owned a sheep. His white hair, falling about his shoulders, and his flowing white beard, seemed made for a red suit and Christmas carols. He was a kindly old man, but it was said in Stauffer that he was not quite right in the head. Even though he lived far back in the hills where wild animals abounded, his only weapon was the shepherd's crook. His home was a cabin at the head of a creek known as Roaring Branch. During the summer, he ranged the hills, hunting ginseng, golden seal, and other medicinal plants for which there was a market, and if he were in the right mood, he could be hired for an occasional odd job. But he would go nowhere unless his dog was also welcome.

His taste in dogs was startling! He never owned a small one, possibly he thought big dogs better fitted the big hills he loved so well. He understood and loved his dogs, and, in turn, was adored by them, and perhaps that was a sort of compensation. He did not understand his fellow men nor did they understand him.

The dog that walked into the village with him was huge. The predominant strain was shepherd, but it had a dash of another breed, probably wolfhound, that had given it added size and weight. Still young, it retained all a puppy's eager friendliness and some puppy clumsiness. Its tail never seemed to stop wagging.

The first person who saw the pair was Arnold Peterson, a stonemason, who was laying a foundation for a new house on the outskirts of town. Peterson shouted in mock fear, "My gosh, Jed, chain that lion before it kills somebody!"

A few nearby people who had heard Peterson shout were delighted to carry on where he left off—towns the size of Stauffer never have much exciting entertainment. Word spread that Jed Fentress, the gentle old root hunter from the hills, was coming into town with a lion. As man and dog passed down the street, there was more simulated fear of the dog. A few boys worked themselves into a mild hysteria. Whenever any child came near, the "lion" wagged its tail or licked the small face. He was so big that he did not have to rear in order to perform this ceremony.

Jed made a few purchases at the store, packed them into a gunny sack, which he slung over his shoulder, and started back to the hills. Until he was out of sight, good-natured warnings to beware of the lion followed him.

As soon as possible, Jed veered from the highway. He never walked on roads when he could find a trail. Some of the trails he liked were so dim, so well-hidden, they seldom knew any feet besides his and those of wild beasts. He took such a trail today, and sighed happily when he was again in shaded woods.

He understood the hills, and all about them. He read furtive rustlings in the brush as understandingly as residents of Stauffer read their newspapers. He knew the winter's den from which the she-bear, waking lean from her winter's hibernation, took her cubs to meet their world. He could interpret the cries of the hawk, the screams of the jay. The pitch and tone of the wind, the sound of the rain, the formation of the clouds, the actions of birds, all told him secrets hidden from most men.

The touch of the puppy's nose against his hand was something else he understood. The puppy, bubbling with young, curious life, wanted to explore the mountainside. Jed waved his hand.

"All right, Brad. Go ahead and run."

After the gangling young animal had bounded away, the trail pitched up sharply through a laurel and rhododendron thicket. Jed used his shepherd's crook to help him over some rough spots. He was not tired, or even perspiring, because his life had been given to this sort of walking and he was conditioned to it. The trail neared a long-unused tote road, originally built by loggers and still traveled occasionally by people who knew the country's short cuts. Jed hesitated, anxious to preserve his solitude. If some chance wayfarer was on the trail, he would wait and let him go by. But the road was empty. He broke out of the laurel and swung along.

Presently, his keen ears caught a sound that did not fit in, and he stopped to determine what it was. There were a few large trees along both sides of the road, but, for the most part, the forest was a scattering of aspens and brush. Some animal was making a labored way through the brush on the right.

A young deer came in sight, walking slowly and with great effort. Its legs seemed wooden things, moving to the timed turning of a gear. As soon as it crossed the road, it fell, no longer able to walk or even to rise.

Obviously, it had been chased for a very long way by some other animal. Jed gripped his shepherd's crook and faced the direction from which the deer had come.

A gray dog, heavier and older than the puppy that had trotted at Jed's side, came out from the brush. Its eyes were a blaze of fury. A rippling snarl rose in its throat. It snarled

again, crouched, and began to stalk the man that stood between it and the exhausted deer.

Jed swung the shepherd's crook and the wild dog dodged. The man swung again—and desperation laid a despairing hand upon him. Beads of perspiration gleamed on a forehead that had seldom known the sensation. The wild dog sprang and the shepherd's crook swung—swung once more and once more missed.

Two days later, Arnold Peterson, the mason, coming up the lonely road to see if the first yellow lady-slippers were yet in bloom, found the old man. It was obvious to Peterson that Jed had been attacked by a vicious dog, and the mason remembered the dog that had come into Stauffer with the root hunter. Hadn't it been as big as a lion? Hadn't everyone said it looked like a lion, and warned Jed to be careful? What had started as a joke had become grim reality. Beyond a doubt, Jed had been killed by his own dog. Everybody had always said that, some day, one of the monsters he was forever owning would kill him.

Brad had come to Jed's cabin at the head of Roaring Branch while he was still a weanling puppy. From the time he was able to waddle about, he had known no caresses or attentions save those bestowed by the old man of the hills. He worshipped Jed Fentress, and because he did, he wanted nothing more than to please him.

Told he was free to run, after he and Jed had visited Stauffer and caused such a sensation, Brad roamed widely. This section of the hills was familiar to him. However, even if it had been strange country, he would have used a good dog's sense of orientation. Usually, he knew where to find Jed. When he lost him, he simply put his nose to the ground and trailed.

Brad loafed into the spring woods, investigating the many intriguing scents. A doe bounded away and he raced happily after her, never suspecting that he had been deliberately led away from a concealed fawn.

He descended the hill, drank from a spring a cold water that bubbled from beneath a rock, and lay down in the water and let it cover his back. Cooled off, he emerged from the spring and shook himself. A raccoon, faring into this secluded nook by day, was prowling along the rill that flowed away from the spring. Brad pricked his ears, wagged his tail, and approached this interesting stranger. The raccoon ruffled his fur, growled, and dashed forward. Brad yelped and streaked away. He was merely exploring. If there were hostile creatures in this part of the woods, he wanted none of them.

At last, thinking to meet Jed at the cabin, he traveled to where Roaring Branch leaped over rocks and sparkled down riffles on its way to the distant river. He came to the sapling fence that kept deer out of the garden and his ears dropped in disappointment. He knew the old man should have arrived before this, and was disconsolate because he was not there. Brad liked to ramble, but it was comforting to come back to Jed when rambling palled. He drank again and started down the trail by which Jed usually arrived from the tote road.

He came out on the road and, at once, a mighty uneasiness crept over him. The bristles on his neck lifted and he growled. Careful, stiff-legged, he moved forward. Cautiously, he approached old Jed, lying on the ground, and touched him with a gentle nose and lay down beside him. Something, he did not know what, was very wrong.

His nostrils filled with another scent. His hackles rose again and he lifted snarling lips. This other scent was that of the wild dog.

Brad pointed his muzzle at the sky and a sad howl broke from him. He had been surrounded with man's veneer of civilization, but, abruptly, this veneer was broken. He scented violence and, all in a moment, was a wild dog, answering the call of a fierce ancestry, yet unable to forget what still bound him to today. He remained near the body of his dead master, circling around it and off into the woods on either side. His nose gave him the story of what had taken place more clearly than any human eye could have read the tale. The ground where the buck had fallen re-

tained the message of a frightened animal. While old Jed
had vainly battled the wild dog, the buck had gained
strength to go on. The obstacle that had stood between
himself and his intended victim removed, the wild dog
had taken up its interrupted hunt.

Brad knew that the wild dog was bigger and heavier
than he. Uneasy apprehension trembled through him, but
loyalty kept him near that which he loved.

When Arnold Peterson appeared on the road, Brad
faded into a hideout of nearby rhododendrons. Why he
hid he did not know; he had never before hidden from

man. He crouched, flat on the earth, his black nose resting on his extended paws in involuntary obedience to a law he did not understand. Old Jed had been his world. Now that his world had suddenly ended, there was no safety or security and he had been thrown back upon ancient instincts. He watched Arnold Peterson cover old Jed with his jacket. As soon as Peterson left, the dog came out of hiding and smelled around the jacket.

An hour later, he hid again. A half dozen men, accompanied by a small black and white dog, were coming up the road with picks. shovels and rifles. The men dug in the earth and the black and white dog rested in the shade of a tree.

Nothing about the men or the dog escaped Brad. He saw the dog arise in the shade and study the shielding rhododendrons. One of the men stopped digging and looked straight at the hideout. A tremor ran through Brad and the centuries gave him counsel. The actions of the dog and the man told him that his presence was suspected. Suddenly, he was away, streaking through the brush.

Behind him arose a great shouting.

"There he goes!"

"There's the dog that killed Jed!"

"Git him! Git him!"

A rifle cracked and then there was a second shot. Two bullets lanced into the earth beside Brad, and a third clipped a twig above his head. Then something hot and sharp slashed his side. He veered, instinctively putting as much brush as possible between him and the danger. Two more

shots exploded.

Brad ran far, stopping finally in an isolated tangle of laurel. For a while he lay with his body plastered flat along the ground. By and by, he sat up and licked the bullet groove along his ribs.

That night, he left his hiding place and slunk down to a lonely creek to drink. His first instincts and impulses, his first responses to wild law, had been the correct ones. They had guided him safely. Yet, the law that now controlled him could not have full control. Never could he be entirely a wild thing, for he had once known and understood the gentleness of old Jed.

Slowly, always making sure of what lay ahead, Brad went back to the tote road. He threw himself on Jed's grave and wailed his grief at the uncaring stars, while hate of the wild dog mingled with his woe. When he left, a new light burned in his eyes. He knew what must be done, and, in spirit, he was no longer a puppy.

At a strong lope, he struck down a path that led into the back reaches of the hills. The scent of the wild dog lay sharp in his memory. He would recognize that scent if his nose found it again. But with the memory of the wild

dog's scent lay apprehension—the wild dog was powerful and fierce.

Living on rabbits, varying that diet with an occasional woodchuck or muskrat, Brad lay in the thickets all day and came back to the tote road at night. He saw men— and hid from them so successfully that they did not glimpse him again. He did not know that the first aroused determination of the villagers to hunt him down and kill him had begun to die soon after it was born. Neither could he know that, not having seen him since he had fled from old Jed's grave, the villagers had begun to think that a shot had found its mark and that he had died in some lonely place. All Brad knew was that, at length, fewer men came to the hills. Gradually, he began to range more by day.

Six weeks after old Jed's death, Brad came face to face with the gray dog. Dozens of little streams purled through the hills, and he was drinking from one of them when he looked up sharply and saw his enemy across a six-foot rill. The animal snarled and cleared the stream in a single leap.

Brad whirled away. Terror loaned him its speed and he drew ahead. The gray, though big and strong, did not have his prey's young fleetness. Brad raced up two hardwood rises before he discovered that he was no longer pursued.

Spring's green melted into summer's golden-green and, in turn, gave way to autumn's riot of color. The first frost sparkled on the earth and the leaves began to fall. During their mad month, the grouse flew crazily and the north

wind's cold bite was a promise of snow and bitter things to come.

And still Brad, a gentle dog gone wild, continued to range the hills. Experience made him an expert hunter. He knew where the big-footed snowshoe hares gnawed their brush-bordered runs, and where to conceal himself beside the runs so he could make a kill when he pounced. He found the clearings where cottontails shucked their cloak of caution and came to dance when the moon was full. He knew the deer runs, although he seldom bothered to hunt deer. Small game was too abundant and too easy to get.

No longer was he an awkward, loose-skinned pup, with paws too big for his body. He had grown strong and full, and his legs were hard and muscular. His fangs were polished needle points and his jaws were iron-muscled. His eyes were no more the eyes of one man's dog or any man's dog. He had become a wild animal.

But the passage of time did not take the scent of the wild dog from Brad's nostrils. Whenever that scent became strong, he bristled, even in his sleep.

Three times since their first meeting he had met the gray terror. Once the apparition had rushed unexpectedly out of the forest, and again he had saved himself by flight. Twice he had been hunting cottontails in a clearing when the gray dog had appeared. Neither time had there been another desperate race. The gray had learned that Brad could outrun him.

Around the fringes of the wild law lay loyalties the law was unable to overcome. Brad did not recognize them as loyalties, but they often brought him to the leaf-covered mound on the tote road and the cabin at the head of Roaring Branch. The cabin's door had never been locked, and in these months of neglect it had fallen in. Grass grew high in the once neat yard. The garden fence was broken down by raiding deer that had devoured the vegetables there. Brad never slept in the cabin. He had developed a deep-seated distrust of all enclosed places.

Then one night, a howling gale came out of the north. The day had been sunny, almost warm, but at twilight the temperature started a sudden drop that carried it well below the zero mark. In a laurel thicket, where he had sought a refuge from the storm, Brad became restless.

The ancient law of the wild grew weak and thin. He had lived with man and within man's shelter, and gnawing loneliness crept over him. He felt a desperate need for companionship and rose, blinking into the stinging wind and whining softly in his throat. He could not continue to travel alone, and there was only one place to which he could go.

He journeyed through the darkness, unmindful of the snarling wind. He had been living as a wild thing lives, and the wild had provided for him. He was lean, steel-muscled. His coat was thick and heavy, an adequate shield against inclement weather. He crossed ice-locked Roaring Branch and approached the cabin.

Suddenly, he tensed. The wind from the cabin had brought him a hated scent. For a moment he stood quietly, but when he moved again, he went forward. As he had known it would, the gray came out of the cabin to meet him.

They met, two furies almost evenly matched in strength and weight. The gray struck as savagely as a wolf, and his fangs cut a gaping wound on Brad's neck. But as Brad's body had grown, so had his heart and courage. Paws scraped on frozen earth as the gray whimpered and parried.

It was the gray who finally broke and ran. Brad overtook him beside the cabin old Jed Fentress had built. It was very dark in the shadow of the cabin's wall.

Brad alone walked away from the cabin. He went directly to the tote road and old Jed's grave, as though he found it necessary to stop and report. When he left in the dawn, he did not look back.

A farmer, driving along a frozen road far to the south,

came upon a huge dog that had obviously been in a furious battle. The dog backed against a wire fence and made ready to defend himself, but he was too starved and tired to resist strongly, or even to run. The farmer tossed a coat over his head, overpowered him, laid him in the wagon and carried him home and fastened him in a wire run.

For days, Brad lay on a comfortable bed of straw while his wounds healed. This was shelter as he had once known shelter. But the law of the wild was upon him and he would have nothing to do with men.

Daily, the farmer put food in the run and duly Brad retreated until the man was gone.

"Careful!" the farmer's wife warned. "You know nothing about that dog!"

The farmer had heard of a Stauffer dog that had killed his master, but the farmer was not one to jump at conclusions and he had all of old Jed Fentress' understanding for animals. This dog might fit the killer's description, but the farmer did not think he was a killer.

"He'll be all right." The farmer held out his hand. A warning rumbled in Brad's throat and he took it away. "Give him time. He's not ready yet."

It did not seem that Brad would ever be ready.

And then suddenly—as suddenly as he had gone back to the wild and hidden himself away—his memory stirred. The hair-trigger watchfulness, the sense of ever-present danger that was his legacy from dim ages, began to go out of his blood. What came back to him sharply was a memory of one man's kindness.

The farmer brought food and filled Brad's feeding dish. When he looked up, Brad was almost upon him. His body grew rigid.

But today no threat rumbled from the dog's throat. The old law had come to him out of forgotten ages, but kindness had revived a newer law. His tail wagged gently as he laid his head on the farmer's knee.

The Black Horse

THE JULY SUN was hot, and the mountain was high. Jed
Hale brushed the perspiration from his forehead as he
mounted over the top. The coil of rope that was wrapped
around his middle started to chafe. Jed unwrapped it and
threw it on the ground while he sat down to rest.

He chewed thoughtfully on a straw and gazed down
the range of low hills that stretched as far as he could see.
The big, saucerlike hoofmarks of the horse led down, but
there was no particular hurry. The animal was not traveling fast. A man on foot, if he had two good legs, could see
him as many times a day as he chose. But the black horse
could not be caught. Jed had known that when he began.

After an hour, the boy rose to his feet and, at the limp-
ing hobble that was his fastest pace, started down the hill
on the trail of his prey. If he could bring back with him,

something that fifteen men, each mounted on a good saddle horse, had not been able to do, he would get five hundred dollars. Raglan would pay that much for the black.

Jed had seen the wild horse scatter Raglan's men. After two days of constant chasing, they had finally run him into the stout log corral that they had built. The corral had been strong enough to hold any ordinary animal, but the black had crashed through it as though it had been matchwood when they tried to put a rope on him. The man on the wiry saddle pony, who had roped the horse as he ran, had barely escaped with his life. The pony had been dragged along for fifty yards, and would have been killed if the saddle girth had not broken. The black horse had rid himself of the rope in some fashion. It had not been on him when Jed caught up with him.

Jed's crippled leg gave him trouble going downhill. He was glad when he passed the summits of the low hills and descended into the valley, where it was level. There was a stream in the valley. The boy drank, and ate his fill of the ripe raspberries that hung over the water. He had no money to buy supplies to bring along. But he needn't starve. More than once he had lived off the country.

A mile down the valley, he found the black horse. It stood with its head in the shade of a tree, swishing the flies away with its tail. Noiselessly, Jed sank behind a patch of brush, and for four hours lost himself in staring.

It was the biggest and most magnificent horse Jed had ever seen. He knew horses. Son of an indifferent mother and a father who had vanished shortly after he was born,

victim of paralysis in his childhood, he had spent all his
life doing chores for Raglan and other stockmen in the
hills. He had never earned more than ten dollars a month,
but he had dreams and ambitions. If he could get only ten
acres of land for himself, he would somehow or other pro-
cure a mare and make a living raising horses. That, for
Jed, would be all he wanted of happiness.

The hill men said that nobody could capture that wild
horse, nothing could tame it. Every man in the hills had
tried. The black wasn't fast. Three riders besides Raglan's
men had had their ropes on him. Two of them had had
their lassos broken and the third had cut his rather than
risk having his saddle horse dragged to death. Jed looked
at the Manila rope that he had again looped about his waist

and shook his head. It was the best and strongest rope to be had, but it would not hold this untamed creature. Still—Raglan offered five hundred dollars.

Dusk fell. The black horse moved lazily out of the shade of the tree, to begin cropping at the rich grass that grew along the creek. For another half-hour Jed watched him. When his pursuer was near the horse, he was not Jed Hale, crippled chore boy and roustabout. In some mysterious way, he borrowed from the animal's boundless vitality. When the horse grazed too close to him, and there was danger of his being discovered, Jed slipped out of his hiding place and moved half a mile up the valley. There, under the side of a mossy log, he made his bed for the night.

With sunup, he rolled from under the log. He had slept well enough, and he was not tired, but even the summer nights were chilly in the hills. As briskly as he could, he set off down the valley to where he had last seen the horse.

The black was browsing peacefully in the center of the patch of wild grass that grew along the creek. For all the world, he might have been one of Raglan's Percherons, grazing in his home pasture. But he was bigger than any Percheron that Raglan owned. There was another difference, too, a subtle one, not to be noticed by the casual eye. When grazing, the black raised his head at least once every minute to look about him. It was the mark of the wild thing that must be aware of danger; no tame horse did that.

For a quarter of an hour, Jed studied him from the shelter of some aspen trees. Then, as slowly as he could walk, he went into the little field where the horse grazed. As soon as he left the shelter of the trees, the horse stopped grazing and looked at him steadily. Jed's pulse pounded, the veins in his temples throbbed. Men with years more experience than he had said the horse was bad—a natural killer.

Recklessly, Jed walked on. He came to within fifty feet of the horse. He made a nervous little start and trotted a few steps. Jed paused to make soothing noises with his mouth. The rope he had been carrying he threw to the ground. Two yards farther on, the horse stopped and swung his head to look at the crippled boy. Jed advanced another twenty feet.

The black swung about. There was no fear in him, but neither was there any viciousness. His ears tipped forward, not back. His eyes betrayed only a lively curiosity toward this creature that followed him so persistently.

In low tones that scarcely carried across the few feet that separated them, Jed talked to the horse. Still talking, he walked toward him. The black tossed his head in puzzled wonderment and made nervous little motions with his hoofs. Fifteen feet separated the pair, then ten feet. The horse shone like a mountain of muscle and strength. With a sudden blasting snort, he wheeled and thundered down the valley. Jed sank to the ground. Perspiration covered his face. He had done what no other man in the hills had ever done. He had stood unarmed within striking distance of the horse. But this animal was not a killer. If he was Jed knew that he would not be alive now.

35

The boy took a fish line and hook from his pocket and picked some worms from the bottom of an overturned stone. He cut a willow pole with his sheath knife, and caught three trout from the stream. He built a fire and broiled the fish over the flames. It was a fool's mission that he was on. He should be back among the stockmen, earning the money that would provide him with food during the winter to come. Deliberately, he ate the trout. Then, getting to his feet, he put the fire out and struck off in the direction taken by the horse.

For another six days Jed followed the black about the low hills. He rested when the horse rested . . . and went on when the horse moved again. For the six days the animal stayed within a mile's radius of the small meadow where Jed had tried to approach him. Then, on the seventh day, moved by some unaccountable impulse within his massive head, he struck across the low hills and did not stop at any of his customary grazing grounds. Patiently, Jed gathered up his coil of rope and followed. The horse had been foaled in Raglan's back pasture, and had somehow been overlooked in the fall roundup.

They were, Jed guessed, traveling in a great circle and, within a month or six weeks, would come to Raglan's pasture again. It was only at rare intervals that the black horse appeared at the pasture. His visits were alway unwelcome. Numberless times he had lured mares into the hills with him, and only with difficulty had they been recaptured.

All day Jed traveled without stopping. It marked the first day that he did not see the horse. He was a little fear-

ful when he made his bed that night under a ledge of rocks, a dozen miles from where they had started. For two hours, he lay peering into the dark, unable to sleep. He did not own the horse—and could not catch him, and by spending his time following him was only making it certain that he would have to live all next winter on boiled corn meal, when he was lucky enough to get it.

Jed was up the next morning with the first streak of dawn and did not bother with a cooked meal. Some low-hanging Juneberries served him for a breakfast. He ate a few and picked a great handful to eat as he walked. Only when he was again on the trail of the horse did he feel at ease.

At twilight he found the black again. He was quietly grazing in the bottom of a low and rocky ravine. The boy

lay on top of the ravine and watched him. He had never been in this country before, and did not like it. The valleys were not the gently sloping ones of the low hills he had just left. It was a place of rocks, of steep ravines and, oddly enough, swamps. The creeks here were slow and muddy —a good country to stay out of, he decided.

With night, Jed moved a quarter mile back from the lip of the ravine and built a fire. He supped on berries, but rabbit signs were plentiful. With his knife, he cut a yard from the end of his rope and unbraided it. Within a hundred yards of his fire he set a dozen snares, then curled on the ground beside the fire to sleep.

He awoke in the middle of the night. The air was cool. A high wind soared across the rocky ledge upon which he slept. Thunder rolled in the sky. The darkness was made fearfully alight by flashes of lightning. Jed picked up a fat pine knot that dripped sticky pitch and stirred the embers of his fire. He lighted the knot at the embers, and, with it blazing in his hands, he made the rounds of his snares. There were rabbits in two of them. Gathering them up, together with the unsprung snares, he made his way along the rocky ledge by the light of the pine torch.

Halfway around it, he came to the place he sought. Close to the wall of the cliff, a huge boulder lay across two smaller ones. The natural cave thus formed was full of wind-blown leaves. Placing the pair of rabbits on top of the rock, Jed crawled in among the leaves and, in a few seconds, was fast asleep.

The second time Jed awoke in a wet world. Torrential

rain had fallen while he slept. The sluggish stream that he could see from his retreat flowed out of its banks. Every leaf on every tree dripped water. A light rain still fell. Jed shrugged and turned back to the cave. He built a fire in the dry leaves and fed it with wood that he split with his knife so it would burn. When both the rabbits were cooked and eaten, he wound the rope about him and set out to look for the wild horse.

The black was not in the same ravine where Jed had seen him last night. The boy glanced at the steep wall of the ravine, and at the swamp at its mouth. The animal could neither climb one nor cross the other. Jed walked along the edge of the ravine; descending into it when he did not have to would be both hard work and unnecessary. At the head of the ravine, where it ran onto the summit of the hill, he found the horse's tracks. He followed them.

For five miles the black had evidently walked across the level top of the hill. Finally, through a cleft in its rocky side, he had gone down into another of the steep little ravines. There was a trail five feet wide where he had half-walked and half-slid down.

The rain had stopped, but a wind still blew. Jed stood at the top of the path where the horse had gone down and examined it critically. The walls of the ravine were forty feet high and steep. At the bottom, it was scarcely twenty feet across.

Jed worked his way along the rim of the ravine toward the mouth. He would descend into it ahead of the horse and chase him up the ravine to the safe travel on top.

Where the ravine led into the main valley there was another of the dismal swamps, a big one this time, fully a mile across, and it ran as far up and down the main valley as Jed was able to see. The black horse stood at the edge of the swamp pawing the soft ground anxiously with a front hoof. Jed watched as he galloped a few yards up the grass-less floor of the ravine, then turned to test the swamp again.

For the first time since he had been following him, Jed saw the black worried. He peered anxiously about. Some-where in the ravine was an enemy that he could not see. There were rattlesnakes and copperheads to be found in great numbers in just such places, but the wild horse was snake-wise, he could avoid these. Occasionally, a wander-ing cougar was known to cross the hills, and to take a colt or calf from the stockmen's herds. That must be it. A big cougar might possibly be able to fasten itself on the horse's back and to kill it with fangs and claws.

Ten feet below Jed a little ledge jutted out from the side of the ravine. He doubled his rope about a tree and slid down. It was excruciatingly painful work. For several sec-onds after he gained the ledge, he lay gasping for breath.

At a blasting neigh of terror from the horse, he crawled to the edge and looked over. Below him, the black stood with his head thrown erect, his nostrils flaring, and his eyes reflecting the terror they felt. Jed yanked the rope down to him and looped it over a rock. The horse was in danger. He had to get to him. A cougar would run from a man, even such a man as himself.

For fifteen painful feet Jed struggled down the face of

the ravine. His crippled leg sent spasms of pain shooting over his entire body. Grimly he held on. Five more feet he descended. Then his body proved unequal to the task his mind had set it to do. He lost his hold on the rope and landed in a heap at the bottom of the ravine.

He sat up to look about. Ten feet in front of him, the black stood rigid, staring up the ravine.

Jed shook his head to clear it, and took his knife from its sheath. There was no time now for anything save finding and despatching whatever nameless terror beset the horse. He rose to his feet, by sheer will power putting strength into his legs. When he walked up the ravine, he passed so close to the black that he might have reached out and touched him if he had wanted to. The horse merely side-stepped a few paces and followed him with questioning eyes.

The cougar would now either attack or slink away. Walking slowly, searching every ledge with his eyes and missing nothing, Jed advanced. He could not see anything. But there was a sinister thing here that could be neither seen nor heard, only sensed. The air was growing more gushy; pebbles rattled into the ravine. Jed glanced anxiously back over his shoulder. If somehow he had missed the enemy and it had got behind him to attack the horse—But the black stood still; to all appearances he had not moved a muscle.

Suddenly, the silence was broken. The horse screamed, a long and chilling blast of fear. There came the pound of his hoofs as he fled back down the ravine. Jed heard him

44

splashing into the swamp. Simultaneously, there sounded a
deep-throated rumble from up the ravine, when a huge
boulder loosed its hold on the canyon's lip, to thunder
down the side. It gathered others while it rolled. There was
a staccato rattling as shale mingled with the avalanche.

Jed sheathed his knife. Within a minute, everything was
over. A pall of shale dust hung in the ravine, but that was
wafted away by its own weight. The avalanche, then, was
the enemy. Animal instinct had told the horse that the
wind would set the slide off. The ravine was now blocked
by a wall of rock and shale to a third of its height. Great
boulders, that the boy could never move were wedged in
the shale. A man could get over it, but the black horse,
never. With a shrug, Jed turned back to the swamp and
to the horse.

The animal was a raving-mad thing. Ten feet from the

rocky floor of the ravine, he struggled in the grip of the mud that was already up to his belly. His breath came in agonized gasps as he strove with all his mighty strength to free himself of the slimy hand of the swamp. Slowly, inexorably, he sank. As Jed watched, he flung himself four inches out of the slime, then fell back again, to sink deeper.

Jed walked into the swamp. It sucked at his bare feet—and sighed because it could not grip them. If he kept out of holes and stepped on grass tussocks wherever he could, he would not sink.

The black was fast in the grip of the mud when Jed reached his side. He could not move a leg, but still tossed his head wildly. A sublime sense of elation gripped the boy when he first laid a hand on the horse's back. He had, he felt, at last known a full moment in his life.

"Easy, old boy," he crooned. "Take it easy."

The black swung his head about and knocked him sprawling in the mud. Coolly, Jed picked himself up to walk back to the mired animal. Kneeling by the horse's shoulder, he ran his hand slowly up its neck.

"Don't be worried, horse," he pleaded. "Don't fight so, old fellow. I'll get you out."

Wildly the black struggled. Slowly, carefully, making no move that might alarm, Jed scratched his neck and talked to him. Finally, the frantic creature stopped his insane thrashing and held his head still. Calmly, Jed walked to the front of him. Instantly, the horse closed his jaws on the boy's arm. Jed gritted his teeth as the strong teeth squeezed, but his free hand played soothingly around the animal's ears.

The horse unclenched his jaws. He pressed his muzzle against Jed's mud-caked body and smelled him over. The boy grinned happily. The black and he were acquainted. Now he could go to work.

The frenzied flight of the horse had carried him a dozen feet from the floor of the ravine, and left him facing into the swamp. Still keeping up his murmuring undertone, Jed studied the situation. He had no lifts or hoists, and no way of getting any. It was useless for him to try to pit his own strength against the sucking mud. Likewise, there was no way whatever to make this wild creature obey his commands, and first he would have to get him facing back toward the ravine.

With his knife, Jed set to work by the horse's side. When the carpet of grass on top of the mud had been cut away, he could dig faster with his hands—but as soon as he scooped out a handful of mud, another handful seeped in to take its place. He took off his shirt and returned to the ravine, where he filled it with loose shale from the rock slide. As soon as he scooped away a handful of mud he packed the remaining wall with shale. That held. The horse edged against the wall as soon as the boy made enough room for him to move. Jed was much encouraged when dark stopped the work. After eight hours of steady labor, the black had been turned about at least six inches.

In the last faint light of day, the boy returned to the ravine and got the coil of rope. The night would be a bad time. He did not think the horse could sink any deeper, but if he became panicky again, he might easily render useless

all the work done. With his knife, Jed hacked off a dozen slender saplings, and carried them back, along with the coil of rope. The black turned his head to watch when his rescuer started back to where he was; almost it seemed that he was glad of company. Jed threw the saplings down beside the horse. They were to be his bed. The rope he passed about the horse's neck, and made a hackamore that fitted over his jaw. With his head resting on the horse's back, he lay down on the saplings. The end of the rope was in his hand. If the black should start to sink, he would hold his head up as long as he could.

All night long, Jed talked to the mired horse, calling him endearing names, soothing him with a quiet voice whenever he became restless. A full two hours he spent caressing the animal's head with his mud-torn hands. An hour before

49

dawn, he went again to the bottom of the ravine. Light of day was just breaking when he scrambled over the rock slide. He picked a great armful of the wild grass that grew in patches on the other side of the slide and carried it to the horse. Half of it he threw in front of him, but when the animal had eaten that, he took the rest from the boy's hand.

Doggedly Jed set to work with his knife. It was devastatingly slow work—take out as much mud as he could, and pack the sides with shale, over and over again. Heedless of the time, he worked on, making countless trips to the slide for more shale. Before the sun set, the black was again facing toward the ravine. Furiously, he plunged to reach the firm earth. The boy quieted him. The time had not yet come to make the test.

Jed slept again beside the horse. When morning came, he once more scaled the slide to get him grass, feeding him by hand, then he resumed his digging. He worked from a different angle this time. It was scarcely ten feet to stony footing. A yard in front of the mired animal, he set to work clearing the mud way. When he got down to the level of the horse's feet, he filled the hole with rocks and shale, and packed the sides with shale alone. As the day wore on, he gradually worked up to the horse's breast. Two hours before sunset, all was ready.

In front of the black, there was a ramp of shale and rocks, a foot high, a yard long and four feet wide. Jed took the rope, one end of which still formed the hackamore, and ran it into the ravine. He returned to the horse. With his knife and hands, he scraped the mud away from one of his

mired front legs. As soon as the pressure eased, the animal brought the freed leg to rest on the ramp and raised his entire body two inches from the mud.

Jed ran back to the ravine. Taking the rope in both hands, he pulled gently but steadily. The horse fought the rope a minute before he yielded to it. With a prodigious effort, he placed his other forefoot on the ramp, and, arching his back, he sent all the elastic strength of its muscles into his mired rear quarters. The boy heaved mightily on the rope. The black cleared the ramp with both front legs; for the first time his belly was clear of the mud. Jed gritted his teeth and pulled even harder. The horse's hind hoofs slid on the ramp. He leaped and threw himself a yard through the mud. His front feet found a wisp of hard footing. He pawed wildly. A second later, the black scrambled to the stony floor of the ravine.

Jed fell back to the ground and, for a few seconds, yielded to the fatigue that was upon him. He had slept little and eaten nothing in almost three days. Dimly, he was aware of an immense black beast standing over him, pushing him with its muzzle and nibbling him with its lips.

The horse's mane fell about him. Jed grasped it and pulled himself erect. He could not rest—yet. The black followed close behind him. He nickered anxiously when the boy climbed over the slide, and pranced playfully when he came back, his arms laden with wild grass.

Half the grass Jed left on top of the slide, the rest he carried into the ravine with him. He took away the hackamore as the animal ate, and fashioned a breast strap in the end of

the rope. With utter freedom, he dodged under the horse's neck and arranged the crude harness. Then he climbed to the top of the rocks for the rest of the grass.

Jed shook his head worriedly as he surveyed the slide; a good team could not move some of the boulders in it. But perhaps the black—he banished fear from his mind as he hitched the free end of the rope about one of the boulders and, with the grass in his arms, went to the head of the horse.

He patted the mud-caked muzzle as the animal pulled at the hay in his arms. Slowly, he backed away. The horse followed and the rope stretched taut. The black stopped and swung his head as he edged nervously sidewise. Jed gasped. If the horse fought the harness now, he could never get it on him again—and he could never get him out of the ravine! Jed stepped close to the troubled animal.

"This way, horse," he murmured. "Look this way. You can do it, horse. Come this way."

He stepped back again, the grass held out invitingly. The black trembled . . . and took a step forward. Pebbles flew from beneath his hoofs as he gave all his enormous strength to the task in hand. The tight rope hummed. The boulder moved an inch—six inches. Then, in a steady creeping that did not stop at all, it came away from the pile.

A week later, a great black horse appeared in the upper pasture where Tom Raglan was counting his colts. The horse stopped while the tiny, emaciated figure of a young boy slid from his back. Incredulously, Raglan approached them. The horse stood fearlessly behind his wasted companion.

"You got him, Jed," Raglan said.

Raglan was no waster of words, but words were not needed. He was unable to tear his eyes away from the horse's massive legs, his splendid head, his flawless body, all the qualities that had here combined to form the perfect living thing.

"I got him, Tom," Jed Hale said, "and I brought him back like I said I would."

Raglan coughed hesitantly. Above all else, he was a horseman. There was no need for the boy to tell him of the chase, or how the horse had been captured. Jed's sunk-

55

en eyes, his skeleton body, his tattered clothes, the fingers from which the nails had been torn, told the story for those who could read. There was a world of difference between himself, the successful stockman, and Jed, the crippled stable hand. But they were brothers by a common bond—the love of a good horse. Raglan coughed again. Jed had indeed brought the horse back, but, by all the rules known, the black could only belong to one man, the man who had brought him back.

"Jed," Raglan said slowly, "I never went back on my word yet, and I'll stick by the bargain I made. But that horse is no good to me." Jed stood without speaking.

"He'd kill anybody except you that tried to monkey 'round him," Raglan continued. "I can't risk that. But I'll go a long way to get his blood in my stock. Now there's a house and barn in my north pasture. I'll give both of them to you, along with fifty acres of ground, if you'll take that horse up there and let me turn my best mares in with him. I can pay you thirty dollars a month, and you can keep every seventh colt. Do you think you'd just as soon do that as have the five hundred?"

Jed Hale gasped and put a hand against the horse's withers to steady himself. The black laid his muzzle against the boy's shoulder. Jed encircled it with an arm. The black horse, the horse that could do anything, was his now. It was a little too much to stand all at once. . . . Suddenly, Jed remembered that he was now a hard-boiled stock owner.

"Why, yes," he said finally. "If that's the way you'd rather have it, Tom, yes. I guess I'd just as soon."

The Lake and the Lonely Exiles

Tʜᴇ ɴᴇᴡ ᴅᴀʏ and a gentle wind arrived together. For a time, the breeze practiced caution, plucking tentatively at this or that, as though teaching itself what to do with a strength as yet unfamiliar and untried. Then, as the dim gray light in the early morning sky flexed its own sinews and found force within them, the wind rushed at the tules and set them dancing.

A shimmering girdle that started at the water's edge and ended where the shallows flirted with the green depths, the belt of bulrushes kept the lake's middle tight and slender. The tules' width varied from as much as fifteen to as few as three feet, and the shallows varied accordingly. The rushes could not plant their roots where the water was too deep. The tules, the lake, the softly rising slopes around them, and the sky-probing peaks that walled everything in, disdained any pattern and flouted all conformity, but the effect was rhythmic and all the more pleasing.

A half mile wide by a mile and a half long, the mirror-smooth face that the lake had worn all night became a succession of ripples as the little wind found the daring to stray over it. A flock of coots that had spent the night on open water began darting swiftly and erratically about. The tiny ripples revived in each anxious memories of calm water churned to sudden anger, and brought the thought that it would be wise to do all that needed doing before the ripples became surging waves that would drive them to shelter.

Here and there, lazily-rising trout broke water, lured by the hope of finding food, since there would be no insects until the sun rose high enough to warm the haunts in which they had shivered since sundown and gave them back their wings. Near the tules, nesting mallards were almost frantically scurrying about while time worked against them. They must hurry. If the eggs in hidden nests became cold, the young within them would die without ever cracking the shells.

Occasionally, the ripples on the surface were shattered or crossed by a curling V-wake that marked the watery trail of a swimming muskrat. At the far north end of the lake, a lithe doe, who had left her dappled fawn hidden in a thicket, sipped, raised a nervous head to look, and lowered it to sip again. As though his last dark deed, the murder of a nesting mallard, could not abide the light, a snake-thin mink looked for a den in which he might lie up and found one in a hollow stump. Two crows, busily trying to pick up a dead fish that floated with white belly upward, cawed their disappointment or rising excitement as their fortunes waned or rose. Saucy, red-winged blackbirds tilted on bending rushes and whistled defiance to the rest of the world.

Deep in the thick rushes, where he had hidden himself at sunset, the great white-throated gander had come awake with the first pale hint of dawn but, as yet, he had not moved. Then the wind set the tules to quivering and the water to rippling. With wisdom his birthright and experience his teacher, the wild goose conformed.

While all else was still, he had held still. Now that there was motion, he bobbed back and forth, precisely as the anchored nest of grebe, which the gander realized he resembled, would bob. When he knew he could do so safely, he would go out to feed. Until he was sure, he would stay exactly as he was. It was the ultimate in caution, even for a wild goose, but there were sound reasons why all risks must be avoided.

For the past four seasons, the gander had winged south with his flock, making the long journey from summer nesting to winter feeding grounds and learning firsthand of the many perils along the way. Times without number, he had seen geese in mid-flight fold suddenly-limp wings and tumble, end over end, when a shotgun blasted from some hidden blind or camouflaged pit. He knew the poacher's nets and snares, and, from this knowledge, he had taught himself how to find places in which danger did not lurk. The centers of wooded swamps whose snarled thickets and treacherous sink holes were shunned by even the hardiest hunter, and isolated little potholes where food was available but which were almost never considered as a place to hunt geese, were safest.

This would have been the gander's fourth season in the nesting grounds, if he had not made an error that was not justly his fault. There was a pothole south of the lake, one he knew and always visited, where he had never run into trouble. Nor would there have been any this time if, just as the gander was settling to come into it, flying at treetop level, a poacher with a ready shotgun, a one-in-a-million coincidence, had not happened to be walking in the forest at that time.

When the shotgun blasted, the gander's flight mates rose on strong wings, while he himself beat fumblingly into the air. The two or three pellets in his body were painful, but the erratic charge that had found his right wing was crippling. By some miracle, the single sliver of bone that had not broken on impact did not snap until just after he landed on the lake.

Now he was robbed of flight, his only positive assurance that he need fear nothing if he saw it first. Until he could fly again, he was a prisoner on the lake and he did not like it. Although the tules offered a good hiding place, they were no barrier at all to a man in a boat, or even a man on foot, if he cared to undergo a soaking.

To risk being seen was to risk death, therefore the wild goose must not be seen. Only when there was no longer even a faint doubt that the lake was not under observation of human eyes did the gander swim out to feed.

He was wholly unaware that one pair of eyes singled him out the second he appeared and remained fixed upon him until he went back into the tules.

They belonged to a dog, a woolly creature of many breeds that had obviously run to size but had been bequeathed no special mark of identification. This haphazard animal had the muzzle, stature, ears, tail and pelt of a wolf and resembled a wolf far more than any known dog. Only his troubled eyes, his way of looking about and a pace that no wolf could possibly imitate, were present to refute the villainous form and to say that a true dog lived in the wolf's body.

With his huge frame, the dog would have been a full twenty pounds heavier if properly fed. Starved, his belly was pinched and gaunt and even his soft fur did not hide slatted ribs. Nevertheless, the look he turned on the gander was wholly wistful, with no taint of the lustful. The dog's story was just another tragedy among innumerable similar cases that are seldom brought to light because the principals involved cannot tell their own stories.

Now three years old, since puppy days the dog had been the trusted friend and companion of an understanding farmer who never failed to grin when someone pointed out a wolfish look. It was always amusing to meet anyone so blind that he could not see the sham or discover the dog. Suddenly prosperous by reason of inherited wealth, the farmer promptly decided to give himself the vacation that had always haunted his dreams.

Leaving his farm in care of a hired manager who knew all he should about farming but nothing about dogs, the farmer went his way. Neither attracted nor repelled by the dog, the manager was satisfied to consider him as just another farm animal until hysteria erupted. A sheep-killing dog appeared among neighboring flocks. The inevitable eyewitness who hadn't seen anything in true perspective positively identified the wolflike dog as the culprit. Thereafter, the manager was bombarded by threats, which included everything from legal to vigilante action, unless he disposed of the "killer."

Terrified to keep the dog, but equally afraid to kill him and explain his death to his employer, the manager chose the only alternative he saw open. Taking the trusting animal in his pickup truck, he drove as far as a wheeled vehicle could be driven into the wilderness and kicked him out. Thus his conscience would be clear when he said he had not killed the dog and there would be no feelings of guilt when he declared that he had not seen him around the place for some time. Let the farmer decide for himself that the creature must have run away.

Although he knew nothing of dogs, the manager was dedicated to a job well done and he intended to do this one well. To keep the dog from ever finding his way home, he abandoned him deep in hunting country so remote that nobody visited it in summer and only the hardy and venturesome dared pit themselves against such a place even during the hunting season. It was thirty-three miles to a paved road by the route they had followed, thirty-eight to a town. The next nearest paved road in any direction lay through wilderness as primitive as it had been before Columbus set sail. A few wandering shepherds grazed their flocks in it, but the only human habitation in an area whose size compared favorably with some smaller states was a lodge that catered to hunters in the fall and fishermen and campers in the spring and summer. Except for Johnny Warner, the crippled caretaker, this lodge was closed all winter.

Bewildered and frightened, sure only that there had been a terrible mistake, the dog ran after the departing truck. But even though desperation loaned wings to his feet as he galloped down the two ruts and grassy crown that served for a road, he was outdistanced in the first three-quarters of a mile.

The dog ran until he could run no more, then slowed to a trot that shortly became a tired walk. He came to another road exactly like the one he was traveling, insofar as it consisted of two ruts separated by a grass-covered crown. The only motor vehicles that could even reach such a place were jeeps and pickups. When hunters killed a buck or bull

elk that must be brought out, they drove as close to it as they could possibly get and thus marked another road. There was a maze of them, all going nowhere.

Without the vaguest idea of the proper direction, the dog followed half a dozen of these trails to blind ends and retraced his steps. The more byways he explored, the more bewildered he grew. Then, cheered by a happy thought that the truck had surely returned and would be waiting for him, he tried to find the place where he had been abandoned, but he was too thoroughly lost by now to do so.

Nor could he stop. Terror mounted as the hours passed and loneliness kept pace. He blundered into unbroken forest, shrinking from sounds he had never heard and shivering with every alien scent. He forced himself on, knowing no other way to leave this horror behind and return to his rightful home. He rested only when sheer exhaustion would let him do nothing else.

That was a month ago, and, even though the dog might have found a way out of the wilderness, he had become afraid to try. He had flung himself ecstatically toward the first human being he ran across. The man, a shepherd, saw only a wolf about to attack his flock. He shot, but fortunately, he was no marksman and the bullet did nothing except plow a bloody furrow across the dog's shoulder. The rifle's blast frightened the forlorn creature and the pain sent him fleeing.

The second shepherd the dog happened across, he viewed from a prudent distance, and when he was once more greeted by a blasting gun, he whirled and ran. When he scented a third shepherd, he turned away without letting himself be seen. Yearning above all else for human companionship, he had avoided men ever since. For some puzzling reason, humans had become enemies and were no longer to be trusted.

The dog had found a living of sorts. Since he had never learned to kill his own meat, he relied principally on wild berries and, on rare occasions, he had been able to gorge himself. For the most part, he was hungry all the time, although once he found the remains of a cougar-slain doe and once he came face to face with a snarling lynx that had just killed a rabbit. The dog was ready to flee until the lynx, astonishingly enough, abandoned his kill and whirled to streak away.

Now the dog studied the crippled gander with wistful eyes and yearning heart. If he could not or dared not find a human being for a companion, he would accept any other nonaggressive substitute and there had been a flock of geese on the farm. Although they had never been especially friendly, neither were they enemies and, in the crippled gander, the dog saw his first positive link with home.

He watched until the wild goose ate his fill and swam back to hide in the tules. Then, rising, he walked slowly to the lake. He cast back and forth until he caught the scent of the hiding gander, then lay down with his head on his paws.

Somehow he must strike up a friendship.

When the crippled gander went back to the rushes, he

followed a safety pattern which he had worked out for himself. He was in danger as long as he stayed on the open lake, but he could not leave until his wing mended and he must eat. But his feeding period could be pared to the barest minimum and the rest of the time he would hide.

He did not return to last night's hiding place. It might have been marked and could now be an ambush, but, again, he sought the very thickest of the tules. Once there, he rested his head on his unhurt wing and moved only as much as that motion harmonized with the moving water and the wind-rustled bulrushes. Much of the time, he was awake and alert, and when he napped, it was slumber so light that the least suspicious noise or motion brought him instantly awake.

He knew at once when the dog came and settled himself at the edge of the tules, but he did not move. The gander had long since learned that panic is folly, and that doing anything at all until one knows exactly what should be done is not wise. Although the dog was scarcely eight feet away, there was no evidence that he had seen the gander and certainly no indication of hostile intentions. Even if there had been, the wild goose had little to fear.

Man was not the only enemy and this was by no means the gander's first encounter with a wolf. He knew the capabilities of predators as thoroughly as he knew the range of a shotgun. Undoubtedly wolves were supreme on land, but, compared with the wild goose, they were fools in the water. If there should be an attack, the gander could easily glide out of the tules while the wolf was crashing through

them. Once on open water, he would be safe enough.

After a few minutes, with the dog not only making no move to attack but none of any kind, the gander relaxed. He curled his head back on his wing, fully alert but expecting nothing. Hunting wolves were not in the habit of lying down so near anything at all if they were interested in catching it.

When twenty minutes passed and the dog made no discernible move, he became a part of things that would bear watching but not necessarily constant scrutiny. The gander napped. Then the dog got up, voiced a doleful little whine and splashed in the water.

The gander's head shot up on a snakey neck. His eyes were bright and searching and his body poised for flight, but he remained still. He had plenty of time and he did not think there would be an attack. If there were, whatever moved so slowly and clumsily was nothing to fear. The wild goose was suddenly curious.

He knew now that it was not a wolf, but something else, that faced him. If it was an enemy he had never seen before, now was the time to study and analyze it so he would be ready when the next one came. If it was no enemy, what could it be?

There sounded a noisy lapping as the dog drank, then a muffled grunt as he lay down in exactly the same place where he had been lying. The gander wondered more and worried less. The longer the dog stayed near, and through his actions disclosed his nature, the less dangerous he seemed.

The next time the wild goose went to feed, the dog had

ceased to be an important factor. He was there, but only as one among many things. Although he would still bear watching, it was no longer a reason for concern. The gander ate his fill and went back to the tules, seeking a place some distance from the one he had left.

A short time later, the dog found him again and lay down on the lake shore, as near as he could comfortably get.

Within three days, the gander had not only accepted the dog as a part of things, but he would have been disturbed if the animal went away. Whenever he returned from feeding, the dog invariably found him and stayed as close as possible until it was again time to feed. He never entered the water. Like all high-country lakes, it was cold. The wild goose was too well insulated to feel it, but it made the dog uncomfortable.

The gander had long since satisfied himself that ordinary precautions for his safety were sufficient and there was no need for extraordinary alertness. Since there had been no hostile move for three days, it was unlikely that there would be any. But, although the wild goose remained at ease as long as he had the open lake before him and the way into it clear, he wanted no acquaintance closer than the one he already had. Seven feet of tules was the least he would tolerate between the dog and himself.

As long as he had that much, the gander was not only satisfied but rather liked the strange relationship. He was gregarious, a bird that must have a family or be of the flock. He was never created to live alone. Since coming to the lake, he had known nothing except loneliness. If the mallard hens would have accepted him, he would have wanted none of them and the darting coots were even less suitable companions. Although the dog was necessarily more alien than anything at all that wore feathers, he still filled, at least in some part, an emptiness that had never afflicted the gander until he found himself alone. Perhaps the dog's almost feverish desire for friendship was sensed and was not without its influence.

The gander knew only that he felt easier by night and more comfortable by day because the dog was there. Formerly, every other living creature on this cold lake must be either an enemy or a nonentity. Anything the wild goose could not overlook he must be ready to foil or fight. He found peace in the very fact that he dared not overlook the dog, yet had no reason to foil or any wish to fight him. If it was a poor substitute for the company he would like to have, it was vastly better than nothing at all.

As the third day drew toward a close, the gander, as usual, ate his fill as swiftly as possible and swam back to the tules. He chose a thicket two hundred yards from the one he had previously occupied and held very still . . . but remained very nervous, until the dog came and lay down on the lake shore.

Reassured, the wild goose let himself nap. It was not a deep or sodden slumber for, even if he would, he could not have slept in such a fashion. All the senses that had kept him alive throughout four danger-laden years were alert and receptive. But not even the gander was capable of detecting the hunter that stalked him this night.

While the bird fed, an otter, hiding in the tules on the opposite side of the lake, had watched him. A veteran of vast experience and such great talent that he almost never failed, the otter plotted his plans with admirable craft.

Having hunted wild geese before, he knew the mettle of his quarry and waited in the tules until darkness hid him. Then he struck out across the lake, his goal the place where

he had seen the gander go into the tules. He pinpointed his target with micrometer precision.

From the very start, he swam gently, his head alone breaking water and the curling V-wake that streamed behind him less noticeable than that which might mark the path of a muskrat. Fifty yards from the tules, he dived, and, so thoroughly had he mastered this style of hunting, that he was guiltless of the least error. The gander first learned of his presence when the otter came up beneath him and took a firm grip with bulldog jaws.

Surprised, but not panicky, the gander fought for his life. Beating it with his wing, he swivelled his neck and hammered his attacker with his bill. The otter closed his eyes and hung on, knowing the game was as good as won and that he needed only to wait for a killing stroke.

The two were so fiercely intent on each other that neither was aware of the dog until he stood beside them. The otter turned from the gander to meet this surprise attack. Finding himself hopelessly outclassed, he did the sensible thing and swam away.

The furious bird was half-raised on the water, ready to meet another attack if one came. He turned to find the dog at his side and was neither alarmed nor surprised. Somehow, he had expected his companion to be there. When the dog went back to the lake shore, the gander slept in the tules, only inches away.

The next morning, when the wild goose went to feed, he discovered that the most-feared of any possibility had become stark reality.

Johnny Warner, caretaker at Ravenswing Lodge in winter and handy man the rest of the time, knew dudes too well to loan support to the theory that they'll believe anything they're told, but not well enough to understand why they'll sometimes accept as purest gospel that which they haven't been told. Half the regular clients of Ravenswing were willing to swear that Johnny's shriveled right leg and crooked spine were the aftermath of losing an argument with a peevish grizzly. The story had never come from Johnny.

However, neither had he ever resorted to convincing vehemence to brand the tale a lie. Glamour was one of the sturdiest pillars that upheld Ravenswing's prosperity, and Johnny was a loyal employee. Actually, he'd been crippled in a routine highway accident.

Before that, Johnny had walked tall and easy among the acknowledged cream of the top guides, probably the world's most exclusive society, even though its doors will open to any doer of deeds—if the deeds are authentic, were done in the field, and will endure favorable comparison with the more astounding achievements ascribed to the heroes of legend. It had been a fine life. But it was all in the past, along with the record bull Johnny got on Slag Mountain. That past was now as dead as the bull. However, although guiding was forever behind, the present was not all black for Johnny. It was no more than slightly shaded in places. So, rather than dwell on his calamities, he counted his blessings.

If he was no longer able to top off the horses he once

rode, he could still get aboard Adolph Hitler, the bony mule who was gentleness personified with Johnny but yielded not even to his namesake in destructive aspirations toward the rest of the world. Johnny not only liked his job but he would have refused to make any change for ten times his wages, if that meant leaving the wild country. He had a good life, a good living, a considerate employer, and, on free days, he could always saddle Adolph Hitler and visit Lost Lake.

It was eight miles as the homing bee flies from Ravens-wing, a puny little jaunt compared with some Johnny had taken but an unfailing adventure. Ravenswing, if one stretched a point, was civilization. But, in the direction of Lost Lake, it was civilization that terminated the second one entered the forest. Johnny was one of the few people who went there at all, and the only regular visitor. Other natives who might have shared it with him were too busy guiding Ravenswing's dudes to spare the time—and the dudes wanted their fishing one of two ways. They'd either sit on Ravenswing's porch and dangle hopeful lines in the little stream that rippled past it, or they'd settle for nothing less than "away back in." A mere eight miles was not back in.

Thus Johnny had the lake and the ride from and to Ravenswing almost to himself, and he loved everything about it. The elk he surprised at their early morning or late evening quests for water were as truly elk as any he'd seen in wilderness so deep that his were the only man's tracks there. The mule deer showed no signs of bowing to Communism or any other corruption. The rabbits, foxes, coyotes—even the mosquitoes—went about their affairs precisely as they had a thousand years ago and would, Johnny hoped, a thousand years hence. Admittedly, there was better fishing. Lost Lake did not produce the monster trout found elsewhere. But the fishing suited Johnny and it was only an anticlimax, anyhow. He rode to Lost Lake because it was like riding back into the life he had known.

Adolph Hitler had brought Johnny here so many times that a bridle and reins were almost superfluous. Of his own accord, he turned aside while a thick hedge of young evergreens stood between them and the lake. He stood patiently while Johnny unsaddled him and exchanged his bridle for a halter and picket rope. Then Adolph grabbed a mouthful of grass and solemnly chewed it. With the trip out, the trip back, and nothing to do in between except eat and rest, Adolph approved of Lost Lake, too.

Johnny hobbled toward the lake. Lacking a better explanation for the tense anticipation that always seized him at this point, he told himself he was getting old and, if there was another reason, the dickens with it anyhow! When he could feel as he did now, he would not probe for reasons. All at the same time this next step was stark drama, tense adventure and exquisite pleasure.

The hundred and some previous times he had visited Lost Lake bore no relation whatever to this time. Johnny's eyes were not the blind—those of some people with 20-20 vision are so—eyes of one who defines monotony as the fourth or fifth time he beholds the same image. Johnny saw the lake as its Designer had intended it to be seen. Even though its physical proportions and surroundings must necessarily maintain a certain rigidity, they were merely the old frame for a constantly new picture.

When the shielding evergreens ended at a treeless little slope that washed its feet in the lake, Johnny dropped to all fours and crawled down a gulley that let him reach the lake unseen. If he had never taken such pains when trying to maneuver some hunter within range of a choice buck or bull, he had never had such reason. Johnny lived to see, but never frighten, whatever was on Lost Lake now and had not been there the last time.

The gulley ended at the tules, which, at this point, were

dense enough to conceal a man but only four feet wide. Moving his body not at all and his head only as much as necessary, Johnny squinted through apertures where the rushes parted enough to give him a view of the lake. Suddenly, he quivered, as though from shock, then froze into rigid stillness.

On the far side of the lake, a little way out from the tules, a mighty gander was feeding. Johnny fixed bewitched eyes upon it. He knew the wild geese and their ways as well as some of Ravenswing's dudes knew their medicine or law, and he loved them a tiny bit more than he loved everything else in the wilderness. Above anything else, wild geese were the tangible expression of the wilderness spirit.

Johnny's eyes missed nothing and his heart told him what no eyes can see. Wild geese never lived on Lost Lake and there was only one reason why the gander was here. He'd been hurt and couldn't fly.

Johnny's eyes grew big with understanding and agony gripped his heart. He saw a kindred spirit, a fellow mortal, which he understood as he had never before understood anything. He too knew what it was to be hurt. He felt an almost desperate compulsion to make the crippled gander know how that had been, and what had come of it.

Then the gander saw him and hid in the bulrushes.

Even though the dog thought much about his old life, and yearned toward it as much as ever, it was obvious that the old life was no more and would not be again. The hostile shepherds who thought he was a wolf had driven a

wedge of fear between him and all humanity.

Since he could not have what he most wanted, the dog made the most of what he had. Denied a return to old ways, as long as the gander remained his friend, he would adapt himself to the new.

As a pupil of the most stern and demanding teacher, he had already learned much. Although any self-respecting coyote would sneer at his efforts and lack of skill, experience had guided him to the meadow paths and forest runways where stupid, blundering and headstrong game proved as satisfactorily edible as any other kind when it was ambushed or caught. By no means was it a horn of plenty. The dog was still gaunt and still looked to other than meat for much of his food, but he had enlarged his sources. In addition to wild fruits, he had discovered that certain roots, bulbs, and even shoots of tender grass, are nourishing, though rather impalatable. He had learned that dead fish invariably float up against the outer rim of tules and may be retrieved by anything willing to swim for its dinner.

A far cry from the efficient killing machine which any wild carnivore must become if it expects to survive, the dog was equally far from the woebegone waif that had been cast adrift in the wilderness. No longer completely helpless, he was able to sustain himself in the lavish abundance of summer's stores.

He could not possibly live through a winter and the crippled gander was inevitably doomed when the lake froze. That was the future, but, since humans are the only creatures cursed with the ability to look ahead, the dog did not worry. It was enough to provide for the moment, and to give every minute not vital for something else to basking in the warm glow of friendship with the wild goose.

Passing time had ripened the bonds between them, so that even the gander had a double reason for feeding as quickly as possible. He wanted to hide in the rushes and to return to the dog. Incapable of reasoning or analysis, and indifferent as to how it was brought about, the dog represented security more certain and powerful than any hiding

place the tules offered. The bird had seen for himself that undesirable prowlers, including a big bear that came striding from the forest, feared the dog and always ran from him.

At first rarely, then more often and now invariably, when night removed the need for hiding, the gander left the rushes and slept on shore beside the dog. It was untroubled sleep, often with his head beneath his wing as the season advanced and the nights turned cold. Under no other conceivable circumstances would he have placed his own security so completely in the care of anything else. But he never doubted he was safe when the dog was near.

Among other things, the dog had discovered for himself that he needn't shrink from anything else and thus was never in danger. Creatures that had seemed the incarnation of ferocity considered him vastly more formidable than he had once thought them.

He had no want of the security which the gander always wanted, but he needed the gander even more than the bird needed him. Without a friend, the dog had nothing. At no time did it occur to him that he had anything to give. He was incapable of supposing that he had earned, or deserved, gratitude. When the otter had seized and would have killed the gander, the dog rushed in for precisely the same reason he would have rushed a raider among the farm's tame geese. They were his to protect and he would be shamefully negligent of duty if he failed to do so.

So the oddly assorted pair lived together, each bolstering the other and both so concerned with the moment that neither had a second thought for the ending summer and the beginning autumn, with nights so cold that each morning's sun glanced in dazzling brilliance from the filigreed jewel work that bedecked every exposed leaf, twig, boulder, and withered grass stalk. Neither could know that a vision of what must follow on the heels of autumn frost sent a reluctant Johnny Warner from his snug room in an outbuilding to the luxurious splendor of Ravenswing's office.

Only a matter of life and death could have forced Johnny to do such a thing. He was always uneasy in the office and felt he did not belong there. With a brief nod to Harry Trull, a licensed guide idling away his time until the first elk hunters arrived, the day after tomorrow, he addressed Ravenswing's owner, "I'd like to have tomorrow off."

"Why, Johnny?"

"There's a gander, a big one, on Lost Lake. He's crippled and can't fly. I'll try to catch him, but if I can't I must shoot him. I'll leave no gander to the death he'll find in the ice."

"Go ahead." For a moment Johnny forgot that he was in the August Presence and remembered only that The Supreme Chief of Ravenswing loved all the things he loved. "Go ahead, Johnny."

Famous for never making a fast move if a slow one would serve, Adolph Hitler was capable of astonishing speed and he was using all of it now. It wasn't his idea, but there was no denying the maniac who sat his saddle and exhorted him to go even faster. Johnny Warner was in-

deed both maniacal and raging.

He should have known better, he accused himself bitterly. Since discovering the gander, he had halted his visits to Lost Lake at the final belt of pines, and confined his looking to whatever could be seen with binoculars. He had sacrificed so vastly because he would not frighten the gander.

Then he had been stupid enough to tell all about him with Harry Trull both in hearing and in idleness. As he leaned over Adolph's skinny neck and implored still more speed, Johnny could think only that both Harry and a shotgun had been missing since dawn. In imagination, he saw the guide going down to the lake, searching the rushes —no difficult job since the frost had withered them—and shooting the crippled gander where he found it. Although he himself planned to shoot it if he was unable to catch it, somehow his shot wouldn't be murder and Harry's would. The wild goose deserved better than that.

What Johnny saw in imagination, the dog scented, then saw, in fact. He was at once alert and alarmed. Since Johnny Warner had not come near enough to let the dog catch his scent, he knew of no human who had visited Lost Lake all summer long. One was coming now, and although the mere smell of a man roused a whole array of thoughts and desires that were never absent, bitter experience advised caution.

Glancing at his friend, the dog saw that the gander was also alert. The frost-shriveled tules were a pathetic remnant of what they had been. Seared and crisp, some were broken and some lay flat on the water. The best of the few that remained standing offered an inadequate hiding place, but the wild goose was swimming toward some of these. He had no other refuge.

The dog slunk up the hill and hid in a grassy depression. Worried and very nervous, he would have run away if he could have brought himself to leave the gander. He saw Harry Trull working around the lake. Shotgun in hand, he stooped to pick up stones or clods and hurled them into

the few clusters of withered tules too thick for the eyes to penetrate.

The dog whined anxiously and flattened himself a bit more. As the guide came on, the dog followed him with mesmerized eyes.

Slowly but surely, Harry Trull came nearer. Still throwing anything he could lay his hands on to flush out whatever might be hiding in the thickest rushes, he was already on the dog's side of the lake and then directly beneath him, on a line with the dog and the gander. Trembling, but hoping to escape notice by lying very still, the dog continued to watch.

Harry Trull stooped for another stone. He threw it into the tules where the gander was hiding. The bird swam desperately into open water and the guide leveled his shotgun. Haunted by memories of the blasts which had been directed at him and that burning furrow across his shoulder, the dog was tempted to run, but he did not. Instead, he leaped on the man, who spun sideways at the impact.

Angrily, the guide raised his weapon once more. This time, it was aimed directly at the dog, which crouched warily a short distance away, making no further attempt to attack.

Suddenly, struck a powerful blow, the shotgun spun out of the guide's hands and bounced on the lake shore.

Rifle in hand, Johnny Warner came from behind the dog and ran down the hill, so close to the animal that they might have touched each other. Knowing the gander had

always stayed on this side of the lake, Johnny had hoped he would still be there and he spared Adolph Hitler nothing. Shooting the gun out of Harry Trull's hands was kindergarten marksmanship for one who couldn't remember when he'd missed a racing buck.

The men met. There was a sharp exchange of angry words, then a distraction that halted even the hot argument.

The wild goose was skimming across the lake, beating both strong wings and rising on them. Made small by distance, he turned to bank into a stronger wind current and whirled so high that the dog could no longer see him. After that, he listened to a defiant honking as the gander winged south.

The next time he thought of the men and glanced toward them, Harry Trull was walking toward his horse and Johnny Warner was looking squarely at the dog. The animal shivered. He had been so fascinated in watching the gander fly away that, almost without realizing it, he had sat up, the better to observe. Now he was in full view of a man and no more than thirty feet from him.

Johnny spoke quietly. "Hi, fella!"

The dog shivered again, still feeling a wild urge to run but somehow unable to do so. Something in Johnny's voice was more powerful than fear. It was a gentle, understanding quality the dog heard before and yearned to hear once more.

Johnny knelt and spoke again. "Come here, fella. I'd like a partner your cut and size. We'll keep each other company this winter."

The dog took one step and halted. Then, no more able to deny the voice that called him than the gander could resist the voice that beckoned him southward, he started again and did not stop until his head was resting on Johnny Warner's knee.

JIM KJELGAARD was born in New York City. Happily enough, he was still in the pre-school age when his father decided to move the family to the Pennsylvania mountains. There young Jim grew up among some of the best hunting and fishing in the United States. He commented: "If I had pursued my scholastic duties as diligently as I did deer, trout, grouse, squirrel, etc., I might have had better report cards!"

Jim Kjelgaard worked at various jobs—trapper, teamster, guide, surveyor, factory worker and laborer. When he was in his late twenties he decided to become a full-time writer. He succeeded in his wish. Several hundred of his short stories and articles and quite a few books for young people have been published.

He indicated his favorite hobbies as hunting, fishing, lifelong interest in conservation, dogs and questing for new stories. He has described some of these searches in this way: "Story hunts have led me from the Atlantic to the Pacific and from the Arctic Circle to Mexico City. Stories, like gold, are where you find them. You may discover one three thousand miles from home or, as in *The Spell of the White Sturgeon* and *Hi Jolly!*, right on your own door step."

SAM SAVITT was born in Pennsylvania. He graduated from Pratt Institute in Brooklyn, New York. During World War II, he served for four and a half years with the U. S. Army engineers in Burma. On returning to civilian life, he began his career as a magazine and book illustrator in New York City. In addition, he paints portraits of horses and dogs that are treasured in homes all over the United States. He has also written several books.

Sam Savitt lives with his wife and two children and assorted livestock on their "One-Horse Farm," in North Salem, New York. Horses are his specialty but he is skilled in capturing the likeness and exact movements of all kinds of animals.